MAISY GOES TO SCHOOL

DIANE LONGO

To order additional copies of this book, contact:
Xlibris
844-714-8691
www.Xlibris.com
Orders@Xlibris.com

ISBN: Softcover   978-1-6641-6097-2
        EBook   978-1-6641-6096-5

Library of Congress Control Number: 2021904133

Print information available on the last page

Rev. date: 03/09/2021

This book is dedicated to my grandchildren who have been my endless sources of love, fun and joy.

the first
day of
school

It is time to get up for school.

GLUE

MATH

HISTORY

Back to School Checklist

- ☐ Books
- ☐ Pencils
- ☐ Backpack
- ☐ Calculator
- ☐ Gym Kit

I hope I am going to like school.

U.R.
TRULY
AMAZ
ING!

I have a new dress and bow to wear for the first day.

I have a new red backpack too.

elementary

SCHOOL DAYS

A B C
School
day

Come on I don't want to be late.

1st Day of School!

Here I go off to school.

A school bus is a fun way to get to school.

I am at school. The teacher is very nice.

Everyone's desk had a book on it.

The teacher said we could read our books.

Back to School

The teacher gave us each a bookmark.

I chewed on my bookmark. That was not good!

The teacher let us write on the
chalkboard. I liked that.

I am getting tired doing all this work.

Yeah! It is snacktime.

I hope we get a yummy snack.

My Favorite Class Is
RECESS

After snacktime we went outside to play.

end of day

GREAT JOB

It is time to go home. Don't forget your backpack!

back

home

I ♥ school

fun

I am back home from school. I had a
great day. I love going to school!

Lightning Source UK Ltd.
Milton Keynes UK
UKHW052225170321
380542UK00003B/92